CREATIVE DIRECTOR: SUSIE GARLAND RICE

LAYOUT: MELANIE LEWALLEN & DAN WATERS

Dalmatian Press owns all art and editorial material.
ISBN: 1-57759-217-4
© 1999 Dalmatian Press. All rights reserved.
Printed and bound in the U.S.A. The DALMATIAN PRESS name,
logo and spotted spine are trademarks of
Dalmatian Press, Franklin, Tennessee 37067.
Written permission must be secured from the publisher
to use or reproduce any part of this book.

10606b/Mother Goose

MOTHER GOOSE

ILLUSTRATED BY
DAVID WARINER

Little Boy Blue,
Come blow your horn!
The sheep's in the meadow,
The cow's in the corn.
Where's the little boy
That looks after the sheep?
He's under the haystack fast asleep.

Little Miss Muffet
Sat on a tuffet,
Eating some curds
and whey;
There came a
great spider,
And sat down
beside her,
And frightened
Miss Muffet away.

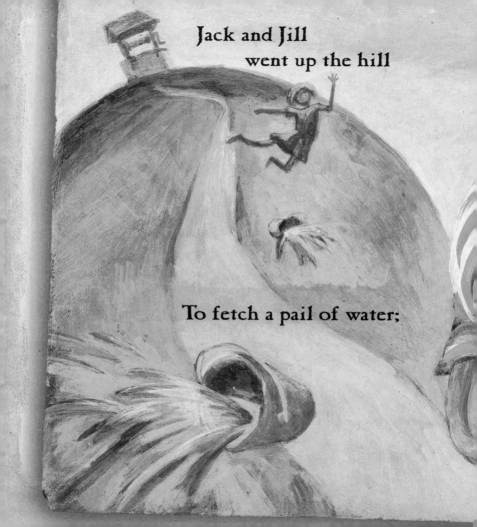

Jack and Jill
went up the hill

To fetch a pail of water;

Jack fell down and
broke his crown.

And Jill came
tumbling after.

Jack, be nimble; Jack, be quick;
Jack, jump over the candlestick.

Peter, Peter, pumpkin eater,
Had a wife and couldn't keep her;
He put her in a pumpkin shell,
And there he kept her very well.

Peter, Peter, pumpkin eater,
Had another, and didn't love her;
Peter learned to read and spell,
And then he loved her very well.

Mary had a little lamb
 With fleece as white as snow.
And everywhere that Mary went
 The lamb was sure to go.

It followed her to school one day--
 That was against the rule.
It made the children laugh and play
 To see a lamb at school.

Hey, diddle, diddle!
The cat and
the fiddle,

The cow jumped over the moon;

The little
dog laughed
To see such
sport,

And the dish
ran away with
the spoon.

Humpty Dumpty sat on a wall,
Humpty Dumpty had a great fall;
All the king's horses
and all the king's men
Couldn't put Humpty Dumpty
together again.

Jack Sprat could eat no fat,
　　His wife could eat no lean;
So 'twixt them both
　　they cleared the cloth
And licked the platter clean.

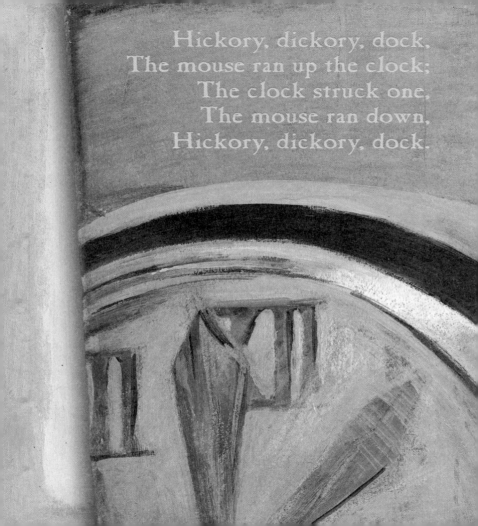

Hickory, dickory, dock,
The mouse ran up the clock;
The clock struck one,
The mouse ran down,
Hickory, dickory, dock.

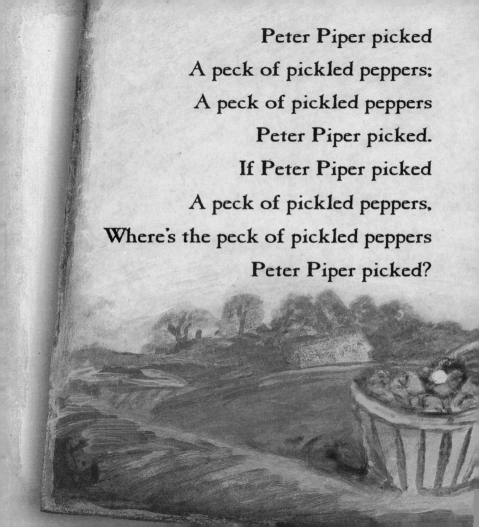

Peter Piper picked
A peck of pickled peppers;
A peck of pickled peppers
Peter Piper picked.
If Peter Piper picked
A peck of pickled peppers,
Where's the peck of pickled peppers
Peter Piper picked?

Little Bo-Peep
has lost her sheep,
And can't tell where to find them;

Leave them alone,
and they'll come home,
Wagging their tails behind them.

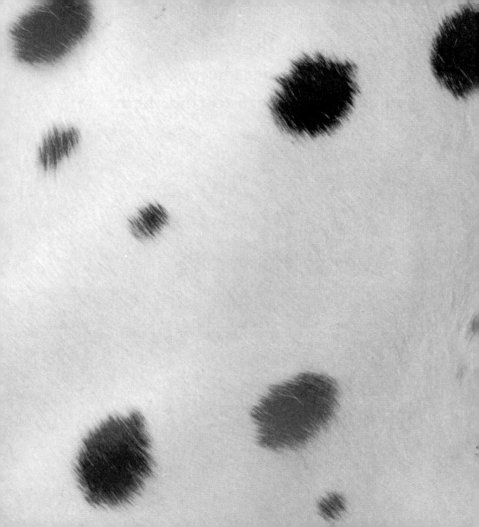